I0607772

**Praise for R. M. Kozan**

"Kozan is a truly creative writer who brings to life real characters across a blazing backdrop of imagination."
　　　　- Sylvia Anderson, co-creator of *Space: 1999*

"... profoundly truthful..."
　　　　- Robert E. Wood, author of
　　　　*Destination:Moonbase Alpha*

"... displays a masterful use of language..."
　　　　- Literary Titan

Other Fresh Blue Ink titles by
**R. M. Kozan**

*Breakaway:1977* (2013)

*The Voyages of Ralf, Vol. 1: The Arc of Purchaser* (2020)

*The New Planet Policy* (2024)

# SPACE LIZARDS OF CANADA

R. M. Kozan

*Fresh Blue Ink*
Ottawa

Fresh Blue Ink
is an imprint of Fresh Blue, Inc.
Ottawa, ON

www.FreshBlueInk.ca

Paperback ISBN: 978-0-9920119-8-7

Cover illustration © 2025 Fresh Blue Inc.

First edition: June 2025

# SPACE LIZARDS OF CANADA

# 1. Orange Oblivion
by R. M. Kozan

I am awake at four in the morning. It is too early for the birds to begin their concert. There is one avian of unknown origin who sings brilliantly long lines of melody into my unappreciative ears every morning at half past five. Presently, while I lie here, thinking bad thoughts about that warbler, it still has another ninety minutes of slumber to enjoy in its nest.

It is not as if I have woken up from a bad dream. The pictures from my subconscious mind are draining away rapidly. They do not leave any lasting impression on me. I was somewhere with someone, looking at something.

Maybe the space felt familiar, but dreams can fool you with detailed architectural realities that seem obviously long known, but upon wakening, are revealed as novel and imagined. I never lived there, you remember, I've never been there, or known those people. All that seeming reality is scrubbed from the mind as nonchalantly as the wrappers from a fast food meal slid off a tray and past the flipper lid of the big plastic garbage receptacle, as provided by the establishment. You are done. No ceremony. Next. I am left staring at my greasy tray wondering what I ate, if I ate anything at all. I remember the wrappers, I do not recall the meal. Yet I am still hungry.

I want to go back to sleep. It is unlikely to occur.

1

Luckily, there is enough time to lie here and think about all the things I need to do today. And all the things I should have done yesterday. And to worry about all the things I did do yesterday. And to worry about all the things I will not be able to do today.

I manage to resolve a few problems in my head, but I uncover a large number of wilier issues. My brain works furiously, as active as the full REM blast of dreamy brain activity. The difference is: I am not passively reviewing a transmission of divergent images from my unconscious; I am talking to myself, words are addressed and weighed, rebutted and redressed. Lists are made, arguments constructed. After twenty minutes of inner chatter, I am exhausted.

Did I say I was lucky to have time for this thorough and enervating review? I may have been mistaken.

I understand you cannot talk yourself to sleep. I quiet my mental voice. I will sip more of the colours and shapes from the deepest brain. I must not try. I must submerge myself in the natural flow of a brain relaxing.

I see some orange with a few dots in it. Is it the surface of Io? The colour of my mother's kitchen from 1975? Stop talking! It is acceptable to go to Io, or to the kitchen, but it is not helpful to internally enunciate either option. It is just some orange with a few dots in it.

It is quiet outside now. I think it was traffic noise

that woke me, some errant horn. I close the window. The room is cool enough now to sleep in. The heat of the day has by now completed its seepage to rejoin the immense and untamed torrents of air outside the house. It is windier now. I can hear the gentle buffeting of the structure by the lapping flourishes of unruly atmospheric gases. A whoosh as it pushes against the nearest wall, a creak next as the wall reacts to the absence of the stimulus that follows.

I think of ocean currents and the orange plane behind my closed eyes begin to swell and crest as if obeying my unspoken command. I will not describe it. It may (it must!) exist without my assistance.

I lose track of my body. Was it gently sliding down the river of orange, a soft citrus reality that seems healthy and clean at the same time? I feel a gentle side to side ebb as I slide deeper. The specks in the orangeness are fewer now. I ignore them.

Instinctively my brain takes charge of the geometry of the situation. I cannot swim so I cannot be floating in this orangeness. I am standing. The fluid field has warped from a two-dimensional sea into a 3D sphere. Orange has become a fruit, not a colour. The final black speck is now a dark nub, recessed into the concavity of the north polar point of an orange. I am the size of an insect, standing upon and looking over the curvature of an immense orange globe. If you look carefully, the surface of the orange reveals itself as dimpled. The black speck at the pole is rough, less interesting, less inviting.

Now I am in a grove of orange trees. There is Scabbers, my mangy pet rabbit. He died of a skin condition when I was very young and I have feared skin creams ever since. Scabbers runs carefree and joyous among the trees and I playfully give chase.

I notice monkeys in the trees. They reach down and try to grab Scabbers and me, but we duck just in time. One of the monkeys has a face I recognize. My boss. He flings some poop at me, and I zig zag effortlessly out of the way. I scoop up Scabbers in my arms and it looks into my eyes. It loves me.

Suddenly we are surrounded by people who are concerned about our complexion. I protest saying "it's simpler than that" over and over, but they hold out jars of skin cream, and then their hands piled high with globs of the goo. I back away. I do not want to be touched.

My clock radio is babbling, the announcer claiming it is now half past six. It seems like only a moment ago I shut the window. Somehow I slept through the concert at half past five.

"I will repeat this, incredible but true. Ten minutes ago, a giant flying saucer full of, what appears to be, bipedal or upright, intelligent creatures, lizard creatures has landed! Their intentions are unknown. We are watching the video feed from the White House lawn, as I am sure many of you are…"

I realize I have never had a pet rabbit.

## 2. Tale of Ill-Ohdor
by Steve Ferguson

I unconsciously kick leaves out of my way as I hurry along the edge of the Quad, quite late, the last leaving a night class. No one is around. I smell something. It is strong but not noxious, sweet and interesting. I turn back and take the few steps down into the Quad proper, scanning the circumferential vegetation. At the back, on the far side, a dull glow exhibits. I walk briskly toward it, marvelling at the strength of the smell such that even the wind does not dilute it. A giant green crystal sits just beside a thick caragana bush. Without really knowing why, I reach out to touch its very clean-looking surface. An electric shock paralyses my body then, and suddenly I don't know where I am. Did I blink, or wake up, or just what happened is not clear.

The Sun is overhead. I assume it is midday. I am in the countryside. How did I get to this rural location? I am beside a tree, at the top of a hill. The green crystal is here, at the summit. I back away slowly. Now it has no smell, and I have no urge to touch it. Below me is a small cluster of buildings, probably a farm operation of some kind. I jog toward it, fearful. There is no cell reception here at all. When I get closer, I see a man is feeding his chickens. It sounds commonplace and ordinary, an idyllic pastoral, but it was all wrong. Every little bit of it. The chickens were not normal barnyard specimens; they were like a bad caricature of chickens: far taller and leaner, muscular perhaps, than I expected. The farmer's clothes look home-made of burlap and something wrapped around his feet passes for shoes. Certainly he doesn't care what he looks like. The house is wrong too; it could never have passed a habitation inspection. There is no glass in the windows and the roof looks like straw.

"Hello!" I call cheerfully. Despite the farmer's odd appearance, I was honestly glad to see someone.

The farmer regarded me carefully. "Good day, sir. Where thee hence?"

"I have no hens," I admitted. This was going to be interesting. "Look, I'm not sure really where I am. Where am I?"

"The Land of Ill-Ohdor for certain."

"I've never heard of that. Is this still Canada, the country, Canada?"

"No sir, that is a strange name. I am not familiar with your accent, nor your style of dress." He peered curiously at my appearance. The nerve.

"Well, is there a Wi-Fi spot anywhere?"

"I cannot say. I do not know a why fie spot."

"This is really the middle of nowhere. No offence. Hmm. Well how do you get in touch with taxis and such?"

"Taxes come here."

"No, taxis, *tax ease*; like an automobile, to take you to the city."

"To the city? No, we do not want to go there."

"What, not even to visit, to see someone?"

"We live here, sir. We do not want to see those in the city."

"Isn't it a bit boring out here, then? Sorry..." I shrugged, then smiled knowingly at the bumpkin, hinting of my own sophisticated enjoyment of bright lights, big city nights. But his eyes just widened in fear.

"No sir, please. We do not want to see the Lizardee. We pay our taxes!" He seemed to be getting quite upset.

"No, no, of course not." I tried to soothe him, but it was going south fast.

"The Lizardee have fully half our yield. We need the medicine again!"

"Right, right." I thought this truly an awkward moment to bring up this whole 'Lizardee' thing, so instead I pressed on with my own more urgent requirements. "Well then, how about about that green crystal on the hill there? What do you know about that? How did it get here?"

"It gets to where it wants to go." The farmer spat the words with apparent loathing. "It is the tool of the Lizardee."

That word again. This guy was a one-note wonder. Well, when in bumpkin, speak bumpkin.

"Be that as it may," said I. "It might be considerably valuable, in my consideration, and I am quite inconvenienced by this entire affair. Might I trouble you then, kind villager, to help me take it to the city?"

"You are quite mad, strange sir. No one wants to go there. It is only when the Lizardee drag them inside that they are truly lost to us. So many have gone. We pay our taxes and we do not cheat, but it is not enough. They want more. You would be very wise to go back to your home, sir, and to stay far away from the city. Why are you not afraid of the Lizardee?"

I had had almost enough of this.

"Look, you're talking like this is some kind of magic crystal. I don't know how I got here and I don't know who these Lizardee are. Do they have a phone? Can they get me a taxi?"

"Your words are mysterious. I saw you fall out of the 'crystal' as you call it, but it is a lizardee stone, and it is strange indeed that you do not know even that."

"A Lizardee stone? What is that?"

The farmer stared at me for a long moment, his expression morphing from fear to a perhaps gentle concern. I had the feeling that many clouds silently passed overhead before he finally spoke again.

"It is how the Lizardee travel; it is how they collect taxes; it is how they steal our young and kidnap trouble-makers." My expression must have remained quite politely blank because he seemed to wait for any change in expression for some time before continuing, this time a little petulantly. "The Lizardee are the rulers of this land."

Oh boy. This guy had some wacky ideas about government. I encouraged him.

"Why don't you overthrow them, you know, have a revolution?"

"The Lizardee are shape-shifting nine-foot lizardmen with the strength of ten, plus they possess great knowledge that gives them powerful magic. As well, they are many in number. We have no chance to oppose them in any way. I wonder where you come from..? Why have you not fallen to them also? I think we were once alone, that is, without the Lizardee, but they destroy our books so it is difficult to know anything." He paused again, almost dreadfully. "If you can escape, you must!"

"Okay, thank you, yes thanks..."

I stumbled away from the farmer, back up the hill. I needed to get away from this madman and then maybe the crystal could provide a clue to what had really happened to me. The crystal was glowing again, but I did not smell anything. I tried one finger against its side. Warm! I wanted to get a grip on it and turn it, so I planted each hand on a side, and boom.

I was back in the Quad. It was now night. Again? Was I back from the other side of the world? It was high noon in, what did he call it, Ill-Ohdor? Suddenly I realized the smell was gone. The crystal was gone too. I was lying on the cold ground, splayed amid crunchy leaves. How embarrassing.

As I brushed myself off with a shudder, I considered that I was perhaps going mad and that this was an experience I doubted I could share with anyone, ever.

### 3. A Chance Meeting
by R. M. Kozan

The small, blue green planet required investigation. The probability that it would one day or might already harbour intelligent life was sufficiently compelling. Benthel prepared to land.

The Botok species of planet Botolko had discovered and catalogued the majority of lifeforms in the galaxy but this was not due to any excess of exploratory energy or hunger for knowledge on their part. In fact, the Botok were an incurious and docile species for whom multitasking was a specific legal sanction, akin to hard labour. What set the Botok apart from the other galactic explorers was their extreme longevity and penchant for long distance travel. Botok lived virtually forever but had an affinity for voyages long enough to be considered multi-generational for any other species.

When a Botok set out on a journey of exploration you could be certain of two things. First, that it would not return for a very very long time. And second, that it would eventually return bearing new information about never-before-seen inhabitants from the farthest reaches of the galaxy.

Benthel was a Botok, but an especially incurious and indolent one. She had previously spent a thousand years studying an anomalous belt of giant asteroids that formed a great parabola around a blue red double star system. Eventually she discovered a form of unicellular life amid the frozen innards of one of the largest chunks of coalesced debris.

For the last several thousand years, however, she had travelled in her star pod through the interstellar dark, the blue green planet getting larger in her telescope every year. Some years she even glanced at it twice, but there were few surprises until she arrived.

Benthel selected a landing site atop a grassy plain, at a temperate mid-latitude of the northern hemisphere. Her initial scans indicated a wealth of animal life, but no clear trace of civilization.

As soon as her pod entered the alien atmosphere, Benthel knew something had gone wrong. The impact of the landing knocked Benthel unconscious, and when she awoke it was clear that her pod was mortally damaged. The sole occupant was fine. It took a lot to injure a Botok.

Benthel rolled back the top of her pod and enjoyed the rays of the alien yellow sun. Botok's original sun had been quite similar. The seasonal variation was not too great on this planet. Benthel observed a rainy season come and go. Then temperatures plummeted and crystalline frozen water covered the ground. In a few months the temperature rose and that ground cover evaporated. As Benthel began her second year on the blue green planet, she had to admit to herself that the cycle of the seasons was much shorter on this planet than on her home world.

The diurnal cycle was also much briefer. Some days

Benthel would have a thought about correcting some system fault in her pod and before she had completed the mental preparation for the work, the sun had already set again. In time, Benthel adapted to the rhythms of the new planet. She would work, observing and thinking, for several days, and then sleep for a similar amount of time. The vapour in the air contained micro-nutrients that both pleased her senses and sustained her bodily systems.

A hundred years passed. During this time, Benthel had been very busy, or at least very busy for a Botok. She had acquired detailed observations of five types of plant life, seventeen types of insects, plus eight types of small animals, four of those being flying creatures. The winged animals were especially fascinating to Benthel. How far could such an animal travel, unaided by mechanical inventions, and how many new things would it see each and every day? The very thought of it simultaneously excited and exhausted Benthel.

Certainly Benthel could have discovered a great deal more had her pod not suffered multiple failures upon landing. As it was, she could observe and record all in view around her but because the pod's terrain interface had been damaged, it could not move from the location where it had come to rest. A liftoff in the future might be possible, the journey home was not ruled out, but the physical damage to the treads and geared mechanics along the underside of the pod were beyond repair, at least any repair that could be done by one Botok on a technology-free alien planet.

This did not upset Benthel. She was patient. If there was intelligent life on this planet, it would eventually find her. There was no rush.

Another thousand years passed. Benthel's archive of observed species continued to grow. There were worms that crawled over the ground and animals that burrowed holes into the trunks of the few large trees scattered sparsely about the grassy plain. There were more of the fascinating flying creatures.

One year, a herd of large herbivores crowded south past her pod, their migration or grazing pattern altered for unknown reasons. The next year they returned, but after that they disappeared again. Perhaps their route took them beyond the edge of the plain, beyond Benthel's sight lines.

Then Benthel began to detect changes in the air composition. The carbon dioxide ratio was up and various contaminants pointed to evidence of industrial processes. Soon intelligent life will find me, thought Benthel.

About fifty sidereal years later, an upright biped wandered into Benthel's field of observation. The creature sported a hunting implement, a long stick with a pointed end. It had paint applied to its face in a geometric pattern and wore a woven cloth over its lower body. Obvious signs of intelligence on display, thought Benthel. Tool-using behaviour and abstract thinking.

The biped seemed to recognize that Benthel was not native to the area. It approached her slowly (that is slowly compared to other animals on this planet, not slowly from a Botok perspective) and even poked her with its stick.

Botok mentally activated her telepathic communicator and engaged the biped with a question.

*Who are you?*

"I am Amaru, the finest hunter of the Mongontho, promised of Edemi, daughter of Chief Anasa. Who or what are you and where are you?"

*I am here. I am inside the giant blue rock you see before you. I cannot leave my home but I have been observing your world for a long time. I seek knowledge and peace.*

"My people have great knowledge. Our shaman understands all plants and animals. We can cure possession and sometimes, water sickness too. But no one has seen a god like you. I am sure I am the first. Why have you selected me to reveal yourself?"

*You shall represent all your people to me. To my kind, you will be the face of this world. Know that I am not a god. I am simply a seeker of knowledge and peace.*

"O great rock, I am honoured to be so chosen. Although my people's knowledge is great, I suspect you have magic and power of which I cannot even dream. Know too that we also are seekers of peace. My brothers and sisters live in villages along the great shore. We trade with our cousins who live many days travel to the south and the north, as well as our cousins who live inland and who do not fish. We do not make war unless we are attacked. We offer you respect and peace."

*Come closer.*

The biped hesitated. There was something sticking out the top of the blue rock that looked somehow softer, more malleable, a branch or tentacle. It moved slowly until it was facing him.

*Come closer still. I wish to see you better and I cannot come to you.*

"I will bring you to my people, creature without a face. We will become friends and sing together. We are all children of the sun. Do you eat fish?"

*A little closer please. I do not eat as you think of it.*

"But still you can appreciate the idea that food taken together creates brotherhood. When you join us you will see that our hearts are open and deserving of the smiles of the gods. We will feast in your honour. We will dance and rejoice. You will hear the laughter of our children."

*One step more, please.*

"Do you accept my invitation? Are you pleased?"

*I am impressed with your outlook. However, my idea of peace does not include singing, dancing, nor laughter of children. I much prefer a long trip, plentiful rest, and a new strand of DNA to contemplate.*

"I do not understand."

The biped was now standing within the spear's length of the blue boulder. The lower parts of the boulder were bizarre, unsettling, a jagged puzzle of odd shaped yet similarly coloured elements that didn't make sense. There was something purposeful about its composition, but the function was not clear. Some of the shapes were distorted as if having fallen from a great height. It was now clear to Amaru that the bulk of the giant blue egg was hidden below years of accumulated soil and dust.

*It is not necessary for you to understand. But there will be much time later to explain.*

Benthel realized that the lifespan of her new discovery was no longer than a brief Botolko holiday. She was glad that his travel pod's manipulators managed to freeze Amaru without any damage. Her stay on the blue green planet had been a little longer than expected due to the transportation snafu, but it had certainly been worth it. Now Benthel was looking forward to some peace and quiet on the trip back to Botok.

Amaru's people found his spear abandoned next to a strange depression in the ground.

Amaru himself, a trace of burgeoning human culture, was a hit back on Botok several thousand years later when Benthel returned.

Other races soon expressed an interest in studying the planet, and new expeditions were launched. One of these originated from the Space Lizard Empire.

## 4. Halfblind, One-Wing, and the Halfwit
by Julie Penfield

One evening Halfblind Squirrel was scavenging for nuts and seeds. Again, and as usual, she had to work late. Her poor vision meant she had to rely upon her nose to guide the quest for sustenance, and this engendered having to stay very late in the park to quest out any tourists, their leavings, or the usual leftover slim pickings. A sunflower seed had fallen behind the first bench leg, a stony protrusion that supported some wooden planks upon which tourists (or 'las gringas' as Halfblind thought to herself) rested during warmer afternoons. Halfblind sniffed carefully.

Days ago, there had been strange activity in the sky. Some new kind of bird had sailed in from far overhead, and peered into the squirrels' secrets places. Then it began to occasionally jet down to scoop someone up unawares and vanish. There were several incidents of plump young ones being targeted but, within a few days, the new birds had disappeared. And the older squirrels now chattered knowingly, reassuring themselves: We are safe until next year.

A quarter peanut remained stuck inside the crevice beside the lateral part of the stone stanchion. Halfblind leaned in to pry it free. A strange feathery feeling ran down her back, and she squirmed around only to see the most feared predator bird ever suggested: the Eagle. But this one had only a single wing. Nonetheless, it batted Halfblind across the face, nearly knocking her unconscious. The second blow did more.

One-Wing Eagle finally had his supper. It was a largish black squirrel, not too young, but still quite tasty. One-Wing had a long night ahead still, hours to be spent hopping across the dusty terrain, instead of skimming across wide expanses in the sovereignty of flight. Distance now the enemy with his one inability: flight. One-Wing had a long journey to complete before sleep. The keen eyes of the eagle function as well from a grounded position, thankfully, and One-Wing was able to locate and identify the local dominant eagle family while at the same time hiding from them. No one expects an eagle on the ground.

The conclusion from the day's observation was that east was the direction to go to find the next cell of eagle civilization. One-Wing had to traverse it by foot. One cannot second guess an accident of birth, One-Wing consoled himself. One day it would find its mate, establish its own cell, raise some perfect two-winged eaglets and finally be able to accept his one crucial difference from the others.

As the shot rang out, the eagle collapsed. Mort giggled churlishly and felt the cold encroachment of some spittle navigating the oxbow of his upper chin area. Gosh dammit, he thought as he prodded the carcass with his pellet gun, roughly inspecting his new trophy, what good is an eagle with only one wing?

Before Mort could throw the limp and cooling eagle into the nearby gently burbling stream, the air crackled with a matter displacement beam. Space lizards prefer solitary animals engaged in cruelty to fill their never-ending need for live test subjects back on Lizardee.

## 5. The Other Green Party
by Jibby Schaupp

There really is only one way to quit heroin. You have to be in control of yourself and your life. Take a look at me. I smoke cigarettes and dope everyday. The first thing I have to do is cut back on the dope. It only makes me want the heroin more. It is all part of the same thing, this giant dysfunctional life that has taken over my apartment. If you don't score the dope, you don't score the heroin. But I've been known to pop over there very late in the month, to borrow a cig. What does it matter? Cig is a drug that keeps me coming back. If I could quit the cigs, I'd be done with the dope, and that would spell the end of the heroin. Case closed. It is all a matter of control. You open a case or you don't. I've got a case of Coca-Cola. That stuff I'm addicted to, and believe me it isn't pretty. If you add up the calories of even a lowly can-a-day habit, you'd have like an extra ten pounds hanging on you by the end of the year. And it's hard getting exercise when you're addicted to heroin. Standing in the rain, teeth chattering, getting soaked in cold water, waiting for a light to come on in that window across the street that means the connection is home, that's not exercise, that's just torture. Should I maybe jog there? I know I jog back. That's my exercise. I do a couple of runs each week, but to the liquor store. Money is pretty tight right now, so I'm not too uptight about vintage. I like a few cheap beer to get me going. Focus the mind, focus on what you want to quit, and when and how you are going to do it. It is all intertwined; habits of a life, life of a habit. Get up, go on the run, get back, hit the sack. What are you going to do? I'm done with it. I will find the Achilles' heel of this habituation. A couple of beers and I'm starting to make progress. Things are much clearer at the beginning of the month. It is at the end of the month, when you don't have a choice, you take what is given you or you get nothing, that is when it becomes more difficult to hold the course, to make the tough decisions. Easier to set something aside, or to substitute, when you are not totally skint. The beginning of the month, my pocket full of government cash, that's when I make the hard choices, like this: spend all your money on beer so you won't have anything left for heroin later. Only with clarity can one make such a decision, trade long-term pain for a weekend of pleasure, all the while knowing that you are doing yourself a favour, not matter how backhanded. Of course the problem with beer is that it is an inhibition-disinhibitor, so once you start on that eighth beer, you're digging into the cigs and planning on buying more cola and heroin. This is where substitution comes in. At this point you need to go to the stripper bars so that you can spend your money in the champagne room on something healthy, like sniffing the private parts of a pretty stranger. Some people say this is also addictive, but how can you classify something so harmless as addictive? Sex is good for you, right? Really I only go there to help the girls, each one needs a lot of money because they've got problems of their own, not their fault. I like to help. If you see someone you like, it feels good to help, and in this case they are really very appreciative. The only problem is that when all the money is gone, and all the girls have gone, I remember why I found the heroin in the first place: I don't have anyone who cares about me and I do need to blunt that pain. A substitute for care can just be interest, so those sharing their addictions and resources-earmarked-for-addictions-funding can substitute for the friends and lovers that I used to have. I do attain a certain status in my housing project based on this sharing. People know they can come to me for loans and to buy certain things usually unavailable on credit. I'm the guy who can make it happen, and this involves a certain pride. I do believe after I quit heroin I may very well likely get into a less underground approach to helping people. I have often thought I should go into social work or politics. That's what politicians do, isn't it? Help people with their short-term problems while disregarding the longer term implications, and giving the people what they think they want, not what they really need. I have heard that the Green Party is looking for new candidates, people who can work with the Lizardee, and I am nothing if not a facilitator. But I am embarrassed now, I've revealed more of my personality than I am really comfortable with. I am the guy who ensures the party continues. Vote for me.

## 6. French Fries Never Lie
by Brent Dube

I have a childhood friend who ruined my life, well, it wasn't really him but rather the things I found out by hanging around with him. He was the favoured child on my block. This was the 1970s and kids were running around my neighbourhood screaming their heads off and leaving their bikes on random lawns while they chased bugs, birds, squirrels, each other, whatever. Young Todd (yes, I was young too) had golden blond hair and a disarmingly open smile. He exuded a type of confidence mixed with a hidden petulant malice which was good fun in my eyes at the time.

One thinks of childhood as a time of innocence and perhaps this was true in my case. My family was well-adjusted, and my life pretty sedate and opportunity-laden. I didn't appreciate it at the time and it wasn't until I met Todd that I began to doubt it. We hatched a plan to run away, and looking back, I am pretty sure it was his idea, as he was the one with the issues, truly.

His family were quite mysterious. His parents seemed much younger than mine. I suspect his Dad had been a hippie; my father had fought in World War Two. A bit of a contrast there. While my folks were very strict, Todd's seemed to be freewheeling, and open to the modern world. While kids were allowed to run rampant through Todd's house, in my parent's home kids played in the backyard or the basement. No child was allowed to sip a sugary drink on our sofa out of a fear of spills, while his parents allowed Silly String fights in the living room.

There was one exception to his parents' lax approach: no one was allowed in his parents' bedroom. This seemed to be the one rule they enforced ruthlessly. One time Todd had been caught exploring the contents of their bedroom dresser and had received a whupping that was unexpectedly ferocious and almost convincing. He was almost convinced not to do it again. The second time, he involved me, of course, and here the trouble started.

It was the first and only night I ever stayed over at Todd's house. We were almost asleep when we heard the noises. We snuck down the hallway to listen at their door and it was otherworldly strange. His Mom was groaning in pain and his father seemed to be torturing her repeatedly, grunting with each blow. This went on for some time before it stopped. When it stopped, we heard someone washing up, and assumed Todd's Dad had killed his Mom, and we crept back to bed fearful. That was when Todd explained what was really going on.

There was a good reason why he was planning to run away. He had been complaining about really nonsensical stuff, like how his parents were strict, and had convinced me to go along with him. How could I not? Each complaint he had about his parents, mine were far worse. If he had to escape, then I had to also.

We planned to take a bus and go to Regina, the capital. Surely there must be someway there for a young boy to enjoy life properly. To that end, we both saved our allowances and collected bottles for the refunds, pooling our resources until we had almost ten dollars. Okay, I contributed about eight dollars. Our plan was to wait until summer and then head out when the weather was good.

Todd explained that night that his parents were not who they seemed to be. The reason they treated their children so badly was that they were not human at all. They had a low body temperature and could shapeshift back into a non-human form. He had seen it through the keyhole on their bedroom door. Todd had heard about these Space Lizards who were slowly, stealthily taking over human civilization, but he didn't believe it until he found out his parents' true nature. He claimed he saw their scaly skin and long tails, their true appearance once, just a night before I stayed over.

The next morning, after Todd told me this, his parents appeared at breakfast fully alive. After consuming bacon and eggs, Todd told me that it was likely what we had heard in the dark was them consuming a non-lizard life-form, which they occasionally do to replenish their alien nutrients. He said we had to make our move fast, else we might wind up being that non-lizard life-form meat they so wished to consume. We played all morning and then in the afternoon a bunch of school chums came over for Todd's birthday party. I was especially excited about being there as I had heard that French fries were going to be served, and I didn't get those at home for some weird health reason I never understood. Here was my chance to indulge! Perhaps the ban at home on fries was because my parents might be Space Lizards too and they cannot digest Earth potatoes. It was a theory, and it was supported when his parents refused to join us in French fry feast. Here was clear proof Space Lizards could not eat fries.

Anyway, I was very disappointed because the limitless fries I was promised were not what I wanted at all. On MY previous birthday, I had had a small order of McDonald's fries (a new restaurant which has great burgers and world famous fries!) as we visited Regina and I had dipped each fry lovingly into the tiny puddle of ketchup I had squeezed out of a little plastic pouch onto a separate serviette at the far side of my tray. It had been wonderful, and I looked forward to a similar experience. My spirit was broken as I saw his Mom handing out bowls of fries to each kid, each bowl laced, criss-crossed, and soaked with the ketchup in a careless and negative manner. How could I eat a bowl of mush that had previously been a wonder of texture and flavour? Maybe this was just the way for his Space Lizard parents to break us apart and destroy our escape plans. It worked.

Todd and I never made our escape. I never got my eight dollars back. Our friendship was over. It was a long time before I could enjoy French fries again.

My parents died in a fiery car crash not long after

that night at Todd's. I always wondered if the reason they were taken was that I was on the verge of discovering their true nature. Now, twenty years later, I am working at a McDonald's, and also studying journalism, but I don't know if the truth will ever come out. Without the evidence of their bodies, there is no way to disprove Todd's theories.

## 7. Truckers
by Charles Prime

I don't usually confront my cousin Juan. He takes me along and I help out, and the less said the better. He says we are moving refugees across the province, and that seems accurate, although who they are and who they are delivered to I don't really know. They seem docile, and the one time I saw inside the semi-trailer, it looked like all females.

This time, however, the stars were sharp and a big falling star streaked across our view as we watched the road.

"Do you think there are aliens out there?" I stuck my neck out on this one, but hoped he'd take it in the easygoing way I'd meant it.

"Sure. But not there. Here. Already here."

"The Greys?"

"No, that's a TV thing. These are upright reptiles. Smart lizards with long fingers. From Canada."

"They come from Canada?"

"No, they come from space. They live in Canada."

"Why Canada?"

"Who knows? Better money laundering rules, access to the underworld. A compliant government."

Juan shrugged.

"How do you know this?"

"I did a job. We were taking these girls to Chiappado, and when we got there, our usual guy was with these tough guys wearing big head rigs, like something that could cover a big reptile head."

"A disguise?"

Juan nodded. "I saw one sitting in another room with its helmet off. Totally reptilian."

"Who did the guy say it was?"

Juan shrugged. "I asked. Like, gave him a look: who're these guys? And he said nothing. Just shook his head a little, almost like he didn't want them to see. He's never been like that. So subservient."

"How many of them were there?"

"Three. One was ....

End of Report on Subject possessing Untoward Knowledge. Subject was deleted immediately upon completion of DNA archive. Hail Gilltron!

## 8. Lizard Privilege
by R. J. Morrison

When I was young, I was always told I was not good enough in all sorts of ways and it pains me to this day, but the real brunt of it I managed to repel: they called me stupid, and that idea itself has proved aerodynamically unsound.

I was the youngest graduate from Elgin to attain a Masters in Post-Quantum Physics way back in the forties. My Doctorate included work on PQ Magnetism which was later awarded a Nobel in the advent of the PQ Fusion Process.

The testing at Vanguard Technology Group for our new sky net control system was another success, and indeed I was a managing director of operations for its roll-out in both England and Germany back then.

I spent several years in VTG, moving from division to division, continent to continent, before I became CTO just last year. In short, I drove many of the PQ and AI efficiencies we now enjoy throughout this planet. I was an aquaduct of innovation!

What you don't know is that (and why!) I always felt an affinity for Pythons or pythons, as I can explain. A very old film by humans portrayed a putative god-like entity who descended to live among them as a fraud and a fake, basically someone who is in way over their head. This parody of a cultural metaphysics impressed me, and it apparently impressed many sceptical or non-religious humans of that time period as well. The group creating the film were called Monty Python and their surname was taken as the nascent uber-language for their artificial intelligence beginning: 'Python'. Adding the fact that this particular animal was cold-blooded, leaves me feeling very brotherly toward that type of creature.

You see, yes I admit I am a Space Lizard, but I don't really believe in all that space politics stuff, or biological mandates or whatever. As I live ninety-nine percent of my life in my human form, I understand the human context, and can tell you that it is not a bad life to live.

As far as the idea of Space Lizards being superior to other species, I think that does not apply to humans. We are all equal in those ways. Sure, my lizard form is stronger and can leap higher, but my human form has an incredible hormonal and emotional advantage. We can say one species is stronger than another and still ensure they are treated as equal individuals in our society. I see no contradiction there.

The need to colonize is not really a thing either. We don't need to go planet to planet. I mean yes the Earth is mostly colonized, but it is benign and the younger ones, such as I was when it all began, now realize the synergies of the two peoples and repudiate the aggressive and narrow ways of the empire, or the old culture. Lizards need space, but space is large, and freeing.

I doubt we are spreading as rapidly anymore.

I think the issue is that once you have offspring in human form, you really have to stick around to explain to them when they start to revert around puberty to their lizard sub-DNA. You can't just leave these kids with no idea of who they are or how their bodies work. So that binds us to this planet.

Once you spend more than fifty percent of your time in another form you really start to lose focus on what is your original form, for most anyway. If your original form is not well-suited for the present planet, then maybe you start to think of the new, local form as your home form, your natural shape, if not your original state. This impact your own self-identity.

Then the politics begin to shift. Local custom becomes more important. Local relationships become paramount. At some point, one wonders, who has colonized who?

Sure yes it was us Lizards who colonized this planet, but with our intentions so good and now being such a perfect adaptation to the local environment, and I mean psychologically as well as physically, which we thank our sub-DNA designers for, we really have created an improved civilization.

Basically, it's a good thing.

### 9. View of a Room
by Lou C. Pattikins

The window frame was cold again. What little light remained was far away, on the other side of the cocoon, and reflected only weakly on the evening landscape. It seemed like nothing but darkness shone back into Win's eyes. I can see, she thought, but only nothing. I can confirm there is nothing.

As always, the day was short and the night was long. The time she had to herself after work was spent at her window, looking out into the swirling mists of the primordial world beyond the cocoon of home. Zen says we must not involve ourselves in the Nature of this World, and our leader is always right. We all know what happened to the dinosaurs, those reptiles who refused to evolve and were destroyed by that meteor strike long ago. Alternately, those who do evolve will survive. That is the lesson and it applies to the servile species as well. Our overlords, including Zen, the government mouthpiece, are our relentless leaders, vigilant in their motionless way, but one wrong move and the tongue silently flicks out and you are in trouble. They do keep watch most carefully.

Space Lizards improve the system by making less and less school for children. Our offspring are ready to begin work sooner and so society can accomplish more toward the common goal. Our overlords must come to understand the world in its true essence and we workers must help them get there. It is a worthy aspiration surely, else why would we do it?

Sometimes Win liked to put her kettle right next to her window and let the steam condense there. Tonight she wrote her own name in that dampness and enjoyed the scene of those letters spelt out over top, or really in front of the entire landscape that was, on rare occasion, visible from her window: the ravine, the soaring bird-things, the foggy forest and swampland only twenty storeys below her. Still, she had never seen it up close. Her friend, Grin, lived on 12 and that seemed a lot lower. Work was far above, sometimes even halfway up the elevator.

Win remembered stories from her parents about the olden days, before the overlords arrived. Things were difficult then and not only because of the initial battle against the overlords, but also because the different tribes of humanity were already and always fighting among themselves. When our overlords landed, they found cooperation with the most powerful tribe of humans and were welcomed by that leader, a pragmatic man who understood how to create the best possible future.

After that, things fell into place rapidly. Wars stopped. Humans were controlled. Output was stabilized. The technology of the overlords allowed humanity to escape a life of living in demolition zones and soon ninety-five percent of humanity was safely inhabiting mile-high skyscraper homes such as Win's. With work, rest, self-care, and all necessities available within the same structure, humanity's new habitats were soon informally called 'cocoons' and the jargon stuck. The outside world was found to be unhealthy and so the population rejected it, and with the permission of the overlords, people signed up for a cocoon and abandoned the chance to be exposed to the risks of the planetary surface.

Win, like all humans, continues to dream and yearn. Presently, she lives on the northwest side of her cocoon. However she has always had a deep desire to obtain a home on the southeast side, a highly enviable position where once can actually see the dying rays of the evening sun and enjoy the glowing horizon which persists past sunset.

To this point in her life, Win has always had to leave home for work, travelling far above her home level, before the Sun had even hinted at rising, and by the time she had returned home, it was far over top the cocoon and her view was dismal, undistinguished shadow. Win had always believed that a bit of evening light would enliven her, perhaps leading to a much higher productivity and start a cascade process of improvements until she had reached the limits of human achievement, perhaps even being promoted to work on a level where the overlords were physically present.

Sometimes humans who worked directly with the overlords and had good ideas just disappear. The rumour is that they have been provided wonderful opportunities off-planet. Certainly, the overlords' transactional nature makes this seem likely. There is much to be proud of with regards to human accomplishment. What we can do in tandem with the overlords is limited only by our imagination.

## 10. Nature Versus Nurture
by Samuel Hulse

W e knew your great grandfather well, young
chipmunk. Let us tell you of him now.

He dreamt beyond his station in life, wanting to live
in the bright dwellings, just like any giant would.
Stripey was vivacious and full of life. His stripe was
incredibly detailed, no foreshadowing pun intended.

He thought of the giant who lives right here as an
evil monster, just as you have. Well, one evening,
Stripey managed to crawl through a rip of the tooth-
grind pain material low on the nearest portal, you
know the one, next to the moving pillar of plenty.

I remind you the ancestors have shown us that when
the freezing blanket arrives, as you will learn is
indeed periodic and regular but so many suns long
that you might even think it permanent, what
happens seems like a young chipmunk's dream,
manna from heaven! This is the time when
wonderful nuts and dried berries might appear atop
the moving pillar of plenty's ever more slippery and
aspirational surface. Many a mark covers every
inch, but receiving its gifts is not a matter of
possession but simply timing. Check early, check
often, is the motto for the cold times. Giants are
unpredictable, even if often inexplicably helpful.

Anyway, I digress. Stripey was inside the cave of
the giants! He was in the realm of eternal light!
(Well it did go out sometimes, but usually lasted

most of the evening!). The insomniac giant who lives there crashed around and tried everything to intimidate, scare, and cajole your grandfather to leave. But it failed, simply driving Stripey to recuse himself of the drama.

As you know, our best defence is finding a place of safety and taking a long daydream there so the predator can move along. Well, later that night, long after dark, we could hear him chipping his sad song, faint and strained through the subterranean light port, seemingly near where he kept his final secret redoubt. Days later, other giants arrived, with a bulky metal monster of speed. They could be heard through that same subterranean port, and that was the last day. After they apparently intervened, Stripey was never heard again. We don't understand why the giant had Stripey taken away, if he survived that long. What was the basis of his fear? It boggles the mind.

Of course you blame our giant. But it is going nowhere. Of course it fills you with hate. Our evil giant has spent generations trying to atone, leaving peanuts out in the yard at the very spot Stripey went missing that fateful night. And of course the pillar of plenty. Of course we understand your pain. You could just say that alien morality is puzzling and try to not let it drive you mad.

But as you now can understand, evil is relative and the giant was defending itself in the gentlest possible way. The peanut-giving had been all altruism. It meant you no harm, but our way is better. We co-exist with giants.

Unseen, behind this conversation between two chipmunks, a pair of Space Lizards rested in the sun, invisible under their microbot-based chameleon sunscreen. One says to the other:

"Somehow these Earth creatures frame how things develop as 'nature versus nurture'. The human in this case thinks he plays the role of nurture, treating animals like little refugees or terrorists, depending on his mood. Shaping them according to his own values. We think this is silly. When we think of you, we play the role of Nature. We think of you as food, and what follows, this is Nature."

And with this, the big Space Lizard pops young Stripey III into its' offspring's mouth who, with one clench, decapitates it.

"Good job!" cried the parent, reinforced in its thinking. Nature versus nurture? Definitely Nature. It just tastes better.

## 11. Surprise, Surprise
by Elizabeth Rose

When my sister came back from the war, she wasn't the same. We just call it 'the war' because there is no sense adding any distinction to it. If we knew what the enemy called themselves or understood any of their language (which there doesn't seem to be any), we would do better. We've seen them use Earth languages, but we have no inkling what their concrete symbolism looks like. Perhaps they have some telepathic capability for use among themselves. It is difficult to disrupt a communication path you don't even understand or recognize. Space lizards are a bitch. The news networks come up with imaginative banners and categorizations: War of the Reptilian Extraterrestrials, Non-Earth Simulcra Insurgency ('nezzie', that was a favourite for the first three months), Invasion of the Traitorous Lizard-people, whatever. To us, it is just war, real, present, inescapable.

We have the ground game mostly under control, but sometimes a missile gets through, perhaps off-course, but enough to flatten a wide area.

But, to re-focus; we were talking about my sister. She's seen it all. Spent her first six-week tour detaining well-placed lizards in New York, spent another tour in Turkey and Spain, third tour was Belarus I think, or possibly Pakistan. I get the order mixed up. New Zealand was in there too. Then, she went off-planet, fighting them at our perimeter, near the Belt, where it is easy to hide and then pick off any newly-arrived interlopers. Going on the offensive was the best thing that could have happened for us, of course. Before that we were just teetering on total dissolution, not knowing who was the real government or even who was a real human. Once we knew they were there and could identify them with a simple, immediate chemical test, the game had changed. Now it was our turn to surprise them.

Surprise, surprise, she liked to say. As if that soothed everything, like a birthday cake of eternal life and free vacations. Don't drink so much, Sis, I would say, and she'd say F you, hoist her glass, as if to cheer me, and say: Surprise surprise. She spent almost 18 months in the Belt.

Surprise, surprise. It meant something far more sinister, a warning that the speaker is capable of actions which would take the observer completely aback by the contrast to previous behaviour or expectation. At first, the lizards had us very surprised, and we did not do well. Now, at this point, they are being surprised by us, continually. We are not the weak humans anymore. My sister helped so much in this goal, but she has been decimated by it somehow.

She takes me to her EMDR sessions where she won't let me leave the room because she doesn't entirely trust the 'therapist'. EMDR is an amazing psychological reprogramming technique whereby activity in one part of the brain seems to stimulate change in another part of the brain. It is deceptively simple, with the 'therapist' moving his hand back and forth, captivating her visual attention, while she must talk through her traumatic memories.

At first she would not talk too specifically. She'd say something like I was on Enceladus and I saw a Space Lizard humanoid die of slow asphyxiation. It was clawing at me, trying to make me understand something. I kept stabbing it. It was unarmed. We don't know why they are on Enceladus. It just seems like death for nothing.

Her therapist would admonish her to quit talking about her ideas, or politics, and talk more about the traumatic memories themselves. He was a gore fanatic. If it bleeds, it leads, he even nudged her once.

She told him about the pillage of the Titan Dome, where some of the lizards had reverted to an almost-alligator-type form, and were ripping humans apart alive. She dwelt on the nature and pitch of the human screaming. Some of the lizards were the standard variety, and with their strong arms how the blood could fly, all depending on the particular motion of the lizard, of which they seemed to have a lot of. Some practised an upward stroke on the jugular, quick and efficient, others started as low as the genitals and performed a significant vivisection. Their claws were razor-sharp, as were the teeth.

Later she told me she had made up that last session, wanting to see if the 'therapist' could determine if she was being truthful. It wasn't long after that final session that she signed up for another tour of duty. Earth Command was happy to have her back to deliver more carnage. Surprise surprise.

## 12. Hallway Justice
### by R. M. Kozan

"Okay," sighed the medical technician adjusting the tube that would feed essential fluid to my body. "Maybe ten minutes."

I wanted to explain myself. Sometimes it takes a lifetime to learn life's lessons. That is me. I spent my youth on a variety of semi-criminal enterprises, and as I developed, so did my deviance from the path of human social expectation. I had my own life to live, and it was nobody else's business. And why would I bend to some rules which I had neither made up nor approved?

It was only as I grew much older that I recognized that most of the malice and danger I felt from other people was in my own head. Those people looking at you in public, they are not seeing you. They are not thinking about you. They are instead, as they do the vast majority of the time, thinking only about themselves.

Even when they insult you, it is only a raw symptom of their own insufficiency within themselves, generally a projection of their own fears about themselves. If they lash out in violence, it is their own life and self that they are attacking; they have become so filled with a powerful hatred for themselves that they must deflect it onto someone else. So it is more appropriate to feel pity than anger at their attacks, assuming you survive.

I have always survived. And I have returned what was given. As I approach the end of my life, I finally have the time and motivation to reconsider exactly what has happened.

Plato seemed to believe that ideas were more important than concrete things, going so far as to consider the stuff of actual physical reality, termed 'phenomena', as a mere shadow of 'Forms'. In modern parlance, his Forms would be equivalent to categories, the organizing principle of our cognition. For Plato, these Forms have a reality of their own, one which is eternal and unchanging, while the actual things stimulating his five senses, were "mere shadows mimicking the Form". His metaphysics placed the non-concrete over the concrete. Earthly manifestations were imperfect, changeable, and perishable, unlike the eternal and perfect Forms.

For Plato the idea of Beauty, for example, is something defined by the universe and existing perfectly and imperishably apart from the physical world. While instances of beauty occur in the real world, they are transitory and imperfect, while the idea of Beauty, its Form or category, was perfect, eternal and immutable.

This is perfectly incorrect and I take instead a firm anti-Platonic view: the Form is a shadow mimicking phenomena. Our ideas are actually very nebulous but also strongly particular to our context.

My idea of Beauty does not concur entirely with

yours. The category of Beautiful is imperfect; it is reductive and is entirely incapable of fully describing any one physical instance of the Form.

And immutable? The root of beauty rises from culture and is as malleable as our other crops have proved, although evolving far more rapidly. Our ideas of beauty mutate with every generation.

The concept of Beauty is a tool of limited use - it can only be properly used when transmitting a sufficiently explanatory meaning to the recipient in that context, under those conditions and preconditions, and so on.

"Okay," the tech repeated, but it still lacked any positivity, offering indifference rather than affirmation, like a police officer acknowledging a detainee's loud and repeated complaint that they will sue. Similarly, it did not impede the soliloquy.

If I say you are beautiful, I am using language to facilitate your understanding of my view, but it has little bearing on whether you are beautiful as considered by another human, or fitting some dictionary definition. A definition which firmly ties you to that label, while satisfying everyone else's inclusions and exclusions to the rule, simply does not exist in the universal. My definition is contingent and vague; it serves only to alert you of my positive disposition toward your salient aspects. I can use more and more words to try to sculpt the perfect definition of beauty as it manifests in you for me, but that only makes the word more particular and ill-suited to other purposes. Does your Beauty exist as a divine eternal apart from the Beauty of a sunset which also exists as a (separate?) divine eternal? What about people who don't like sunsets?

Perhaps everyone has their own set of Forms? If so, Eternity must be populated with more eternal divine Forms than there are molecules in reality. Once we are postulating that more unseen things must exist than seen things, we are far from Occam's Razor, and sunken into a morass requiring a Wittgenstein for extraction.

I take an anti-Platonic view: the Form is a mere shadow mimicking the reality. Our human concepts are simply tools, such ideas can never be or describe perfectly a thing-in-itself. Meaning exists in humans, not as something external, divine and eternal.

Archimedes was even worse. He echoed Plato's affinity for ideas but took it further. For him, only numbers were real. Viewing anything as divine and eternal is a recipe for error, and here it seems to lead to devaluing the actual reality we exist within and lauding something abstract as more important. That cannot end well. Those who are blinded by ideology and refuse to see the nuance and complexity of things-as-they-are, not supposed, will make mistakes and bad choices.

That was me. I had an idea for galactic justice. I had an idea for the hierarchy of souls, with Humans far below Space Lizard. I had the idea of loyalty, but how was I to apply it? Born as a Space Lizard, I came to this planet many years ago and took human form, and created offspring. Now I value these creatures in a way that has finally made me admit all my ideas were ill-conceived. There was no grand idea that could guide my life.

All the signposts on my life journey I ignored. I chose my own path. I turned away from my birth group and took on a new identity. My idea of Love was very human, and had nothing to do with the similar ideas from my home planet. I mean, as far as I know. I arrived on Earth with an adolescent human form, but had been of a similar development stage back home. I was immature in many ways, and perhaps things would have turned out differently had I been properly socialized on my birth planet.

Instead, I had a life of crime and misadventure. At least from the human perspective. In the Space Lizard view, I was quite successful as I had integrated myself into society seamlessly, albeit at a low level. Taking a wife and making babies was fun, and for many years I did not question myself. It was only after humans began making judgements upon me and I saw the impact upon my human family that I began to suspect I was mostly human.

Everything I have done, I have done for Love, but not the grand eternal idea of an abstract Love, but for the actual phenomena of three specific living human beings: Julie, and our two offspring.

"All right," said the tech. "We still need the fluid for sedation, but you have a choice of liquid or gas."
I chose the gas for my final transition. It was orange, almost golden.

## 13. Lovely's People
by Tim Tuttosi

Three thousand habitable worlds in the known universe and I'm stuck on the only one without you. When I signed up for planetary survey I expected hardship, but I did not reckon on the dire effects of psychological isolation. It is easy to forget, when one is surrounded by avatars and data streams, that in fact no one spends any time alone in these, our modern times. Long gone are the days when a short walk could put you into a natural setting far from the eyes and ears of the rest of society.

The closest I've come to being alone since I was five years old are the moments I spend in my freshen box. And often I invite you in so it also, to a large extent, is a shared experience. This eliminates all but the process of elimination itself as a solitary activity. And even so, I usually do peruse data streams (voice command mode) as I eliminate.

Now reality suddenly intrudes as I sit aboard my supra-lightspeed saucer, on a strange planet, all alone.

During the flight here it wasn't so bad. You can't keep the comm signal synced beyond lightspeed anyway. I have had a few days to acclimate to solitude aboard my little scout ship. Landing here, popping the canopy, and drinking in the fresh alien air, but not being able to lock eyes with your avatar, aroused the strangest feeling I've had in all my life.

I'm starting to suspect that what one experiences while completely alone is, to some extent, not real. These moments of extreme beauty, and I must admit this planet, BX3404-02, is esthetically stupefying, seem disconnected from my life, dreamlike, and I am sure, all because there is no sharing, and no real-time feedback, of any of it, with anyone else.

I could fall into a sinkhole and it would take hours for my saucer to signal its uncertainty back to my dispatchers. Possibly another full week might elapse before expensively embarrassing emergency help could arrive. This type of isolation and insecurity is something that explorers learn to accept, but I am not there yet. Nor should I be. This is my first mission beyond our data periphery.

It makes a few minute to gather my courage, then I descend the ladder to the planetary surface. My preliminary scan indicated abundant life here on dash oh two, if I might call it that. The second planet out from the star BX3404, a tiny yellow star statistically unlikely to have any habitable planet, but which somehow defies the odds, is a blue green jewel.

I had landed my saucer on a high elevation plain in the mid-northern latitude, near the middle of a large continent. The weather today is welcoming, the air warm, and the sky clear. A large herd of four-legged herbivores scattered as my saucer descended, and now the only animal life nearby are a few birds. I also note traces of some smaller ground- burrowing creatures. The landscape is flat and visibility is near maximum. But really there is nothing to see.

To me this empty expanse cries out for occupancy. We need to come here, to pave over the grassy inclines, to add walking trails to the forests, to create vast undersea stations for aquaculture. With a land-mass ration of only 30%, the planet's abundant oceans are ripe for food production, while it also still retains enough dry land for habitation and robot fabrication.

As I stand on the plateau, I am awed by the remoteness of the vista. I am the first of my kind to set foot in this place. The few visual scans done remotely prior to landing are travelling back as I write this, but they have not yet reached you.

Your nearest avatar is twenty light-days distant and your physical form, several light-months further than that. How long has it been since we have touched? I remember the last Festival of the Diaspora. You were so beautiful. But it was so long ago. Have we touched since then? I cannot remember. Every night I manipulate your avatar. Every night we share our thought simulations. But it is not the same. I know that the psychologists have a name for this: Avatar Inadequacy Syndrome.

Maybe it is not so modern to want to be able to smell you, to feel you in your own singular body, not dissembled among networks of synth-life, but free of simulation, and plainly biological. I have found myself, these last few days, yearning for just that. If this is considered anti-social, then so be it.

I know the mission specialist selectors would freak if they ever heard these musings. This is not the type of person we want to expose to non-social settings, they would say. Maybe so. Maybe I am the type who needs the opinions of others to keep me in line, who needs constant social feedback to keep my reality centred. But I have to say I am glad to be here. In a sense, it is like I have died and been reborn on this new world as a new person.

I have now spent two days on dash oh two. There is much food here but it grows on the land, not in the sea. The taste makes my mouth sing for joy. I find myself making noises as if having uninhibited sex as I eat! My senses are overwhelmed.

But this is not the most amazing thing. Yesterday I met a native. She approached me slowly and carefully, as if I might be dangerous. She came bearing gifts, a basket of local food. She is younger than me, little more than a teenager, and the hard primitive life on this planet has left her with a well-toned body.

We made friends quickly. I showed her a few of my electronic toys and she was blown away by my strange magic. I gave her a unisex tunic from the saucer and she was delighted beyond measure with its soft fabric and miraculous plastic zipper, changing into it right there in front of me, without an iota of modesty.

I played her some of the softest, gentlest music I could find in my library, and her eyes began to pull me in like black holes. There was no escape, nor did I want there to be. We made love.

This is a female without an avatar web, without any simulated sensory inputs. When you touch her, she feels it instantly as a single entity; her sensations and responses are not uploaded to a multi-fold personality, to slowly spread through a network of proxy consciousness. She is here. It is as simple as that.

Her people know how to grow food on land; they do not consider it wasteful or anti-social. Their language is simple but effective. It did not take my compute-bot long to figure it out, and my skills in Lovely's tongue are rapidly advancing.

I know she is a single organism, non-augmented, fragile, and doomed to a ridiculously brief lifespan. I cannot change that, at least not without changing her. And the rules would not allow that anyway. This planet will be charted by someone other than me, but I'm sure the decision will be made to delay development until a solution can be found for Lovely's people. In the meantime, why should I not enjoy the little time we have together?

I hope you can understand and forgive me. This planet has changed me. Now I feel that this life, the direct experience of a natural undeveloped world, is so much more real than that coddled, technological existence among the Diasporatic Worlds. I doubt the

Survey Commission will understand, or sympathize. This is a risk I will take.

I have disabled the homing beacon in my saucer. I probably have a good twenty years before I have to return for rejuvenation but the punishments to be meted out to me then for my rogue path now cannot exceed the beauty and peace I have found here.

I hope you will find a romantic partner who's cool wit and green skin delight you as much as mine did.

## 14. Lucky Man
### by R. J. Morrison

Stupid MP3s with their low bandwidth tinnitus. I'm listening to a CD-R I burned on my PC of Muddy Waters backed by the guitar of Johnny Winter on the old LP "Second Winter" and it should be funny: 'I Love Everybody', followed by, 'I Hate Everybody'. But the quality is so low it is pissing me off instead of giving me pleasure.

Late afternoon traffic has snarled into a gridlock leaving me stationary, waiting and sweating in my '32 CM Velocity with AWOL air conditioning, ironically immobile in the fast lane on the Queensway. The heat is really oppressive and making my already short temper flame. I don't like the look of that lady in the next vehicle. Her hair style somehow insults me. Of course the middle (slow!?) lane is moving, albeit at snail's pace. Bleeping crustaceans.

I don't have a lot of time to waste. It is almost closing time and I need to get this last paperwork to the law office in North New Kanata. All hell breaks loose whenever staff has to stay past 4:30 PM to receive said paperwork. It's not a joy working for lawyers and this courier job is pretty high up on the totem pole (yeah wiki your totem pole orientation facts, dimbulb).

A burly guy with a baseball cap flies by high in a commercial white van, in tight procession with the unending stream of lucky bastards in the SLOW!?

63

lane like a snake barfing a hill of miscreant fire ants slowly and painfully down my arm. No way I can merge. I sit like an idiot. Damn.

I've had better jobs, been in better places. Always some fool messes it up. I worked for a big name, big deal hotel, you'd recognize the name, as the senior night desk clerk. I worked that shift for weeks and months and years until some starched white shirt in a suit didn't like the way I cancelled his reservation.

He had a three-day stay but only told me to cancel the first day. When the other two nights wound up on his credit card account he wrote a slanderous letter to the hotel's general manager and I was gone before you could say 'so long walk-in refrigerator full of midnight snacks'.

Then there was the time I worked at a gas station for about six months. I was getting to be one of the senior staff when a bunch of cleaning supplies went missing. Because I also ran my own office cleaning company on the side, the blame was quick to settle on me and again out the door I went. Goodbye free midnight oil changes.

The lawsuits I could raise. So many people, each without a stitch of evidence, have caused me problems. I wonder if I have a sign on my forehead: easy mark. The world is pitiless, that's for sure.

I move up a few feet in my lane. Don't see how I won't be late.

I can already imagine the frustrated sighing of the beehive-headed receptionist: "I have to leave on time you know - I can't stick around - I have to pick up my children from daycare!". Like that is my fault. Don't have so many children. Or stay home and raise them yourself.

I hate people who give you their best fake smiles when everything is going swimmingly, and then when a bump in the road comes, are the first to drop the facade and heap blame on an easy scapegoat.

The radio is playing some Sheryl Crow. Must be nice to have the looks and talent to let you slide through life with people throwing themselves at your feet. She's not a bad singer but come on. You'd think she was the Messiah the way some people swoon over her. My little daughter, Karamel, thinks she is the be all and end all. I guess it could be worse. She could like Bif Naked. I like Bif Naked, but not her music.

Last Christmas I gave little Karamel a fifty dollar gift certificate to CD Warehouse. A month went by and then she came crying to me that it was no good, that the store had gone out of business and the certificate was worthless. Well it certainly wasn't worthless when I won it two years ago, and how was I to know they were going to be out of business? Kids are so ungrateful these days.

I roll another ten feet and stop. The radio announcer is reading the news. More people I don't feel sorry for. I'd like to see them try to pay 2600 bucks a month child support, work two part-time jobs, and still manage to come out on top of the provincial air guitar competition. And do I get any gratitude for any of it? Of course not. They always want more more more.

I remember last year there was this family that had a house fire, let's call them the Smiths. They had three kids and their picture was on the news, them looking very sad. We've lost everything. We've got nothing. The littlest child, a boy about ten, was saying that even his bicycle had been incinerated in their attached garage. Of course they had been renting a large home with a two-car garage but could not afford any insurance. Despite that red flag, I thought I could be a bit of a hero to the boy.

Karamel's bike was on my balcony - she had ridden over to my apartment the previous week and I drove her home after getting in a big fight. I had made it clear that her mother's decision to let her ride over by herself was unacceptable. She could have been killed in an accident or kidnapped. Also, I have a hard time hearing my doorbell because of my fondness for loud music, so if 'Mom' doesn't call me on her cell from the car when dropping Karamel off, I might not hear the doorbell.

In this case, my neighbour wound up banging on my door demanding that I let Karamel in before she buzzed everyone else in the building. This was more her mother's fault than Karamel but she must take some responsibility for not standing up to her mother and not demanding to be driven over. So I gave the bike to the little boy. I expected at the least to wind up in the news next to the now smiling kid, with my generosity to him praised as the heroic act it was. I dropped the bike off at the Smith's neighbour, and then nothing.

Three days later there is a small story in the news. People had contributed over twenty thousand dollars to the Smiths! They had received offers of free rent in some new digs, plus a lot of used electronics, furniture, and several bicycles. They actually complained that one of the bikes donated had a bent rim. I had kicked the rim when I told Karamel that her actions were infantile, and that pedalling over to my place that day would be rewarded with confiscation. Unbelievable. The Smiths were too cheap to spend some of their twenty grand on fixing the bent rim. La de da.

My car moves up another five feet. Now the announcer is reading the lottery numbers. Wait, I have a ticket tucked into my visor. I check the numbers. One right. Two right. Three. Four. What the hell? Five. Six!? Six correct numbers means I win big! Whoa. My jaw drops.

This has got to be worth thirty or forty million. I don't think the jackpot had been won for a few weeks. Now the announcer is saying this jackpot is seventy-seven million dollars. For a moment I'm glad my lane is hardly moving. I need time to absorb this.

I can quit my job! I won't have to work again. I can spend more time with Eunice, my waitress girlfriend who's incessant shift work mostly prevents us from seeing each other all week.

She is working at Timmy's right now, so that's the first place I'll go when I get off the stupid, dead snake of a Queensway. I can buy her some nice gifts. Of course I'll buy a new bike for Karamel, and we can spend some more time together too. Her mom won't like that too much, but too bad. I just hope I don't wind up sharing my winnings with her. I suppose I could give her a million or so, but then she'd quit her job and become a monkey on my back. An itchy monkey with scabies. But I can get a personal assistant to deal with her - maybe act an a middleman so I don't have to talk to her at all. That would be great. I'll have to move too. Get a big house and some staff. I can finally focus on my air guitar and take it to the national level!

On the other hand, perhaps I should just take the money and run. Karamel has been poisoned against me by her mother for these last two years and Eunice, although nice, is certainly replaceable. I should just get a plane ticket and head to Mexico. It may be best I don't tell anyone about this win at all.

Now this is strange. The traffic ahead of me hasn't moved for much longer than usual, maybe a full minute. Is there an accident ahead? It is 4:15 in the afternoon on Friday, August 18, 2034, and I am still listening to FM106.9, The Beaver. I'll never forget this moment.

The radio announcer say something about a giant saucer appearing over New York. Information feeds from that city are going dark. Everyone there has disappeared or is dead. Now he's saying the same thing is happening in Toronto. My luck, I win the lottery and the end of the world comes before I can even cash it.

I slip into the bus lane, ignoring an angry squeal of half-worn brakes as a bus driver shakes his fist at me. I am sure there is enough dirt on my rear license plate to prevent his reading it.

I proceed north on the 417 under the Acres Road overpass, past the LRT station  and into the mouth of the Vehicle Transfer Tube. In a moment I should hear a whoosh and find myself twelve kilometres northwest of my previous location. The VTT was a stunning civil achievement and a feeling of almost divine teleportation is the user's usual first  reaction to this high-tech variant of fast transit system. But instead of the almost orgasmic 'whoosh' I get a flash of light, some clicking sounds, then a slight bump as my vehicle slides out, almost entirely decelerated, at an emergency exit not much further up the Ottawa River. What had gone wrong? All the traffic around me was skittering at microspeeds, auto-negotiators trying to park the cars on the side of the roadway.

I see other drivers slumped over their control columns. Unconscious or dead? No matter, they are still blocking my access to the off ramp. I switch to full manual. Traffic is much better. Everyone seems to be dead.

I am making good time now, blasting past many immobile vehicles lining the sides of the Corkstown bypass route, when a small golden saucer lands on the road right in front of me. My car loses power and rolls to a stop. I scramble out, making sure my small handgun, I affectionately call it my Wacked Crackhead Attack Retractor, is nestled in its illegal holster at the small of my back.

The air seems to be crackling with static electricity. A small aperture opens in the saucer and a figure floats out. It looks like one of the overlord aliens from Galactic War III, except with a furry chest. It floats toward me and I can hear a voice in my mind telling me that his people wish me no harm, that everyone is actually okay, but they need to study our planet, and in particular, they want to study me. Something about altruism or empathy, its evolutionary function, and how I am a one-per-planet anomaly that needs to be understood.

The skinny little overlord seemed happy to have found me, like their search had been long and difficult. As it chatters within my mind, I consider that they may have fixed the traffic situation, but they are seriously interfering with my lottery win. If they want help studying altruism, they found the wrong guy. I flick the safety off my gun as soon as it clears the holster and shoot the little green man in the head. The saucer shimmers and disappears and I don't see what happened to that talkative little critter.

Everyone still seems dead. Maybe it lied. Maybe I interrupted its plan. I crawl back into my vehicle. It powers up okay. I smile. Well there may only be one man in the whole world now, but he is lucky indeed. And he has the rest of today off. I hope necrophilia is an acquired taste.

Later, the narrator was sorely disappointed as the first person he bit woke up very angry indeed. Furthermore, by killing the alien emissary, this human dim bulb led Earth to become classified as a 'cultivable planet', thereby giving free rein to other aliens, such as Space Lizards, who have an approved agenda for such planets and beings.

## 15. True Story
### by R. M. Kozan

These papers were found in the office of my staff editor, Regal Morrison. I cannot attest they are true. In fact, they appear to have been fabricated as part of an elaborate ruse.

I met 'Reg', as we call him, many years ago. We met through a now long-defunct website hosting ads for local musicians, professional and amateur. Although I ultimately did not play any gigs with him, Reg and I enjoyed playing music together in our free time on a casual, friendly basis.

Around 2015, I hatched the idea of Space Lizards of Canada as a metaphor for anything that seems to manipulate or control us, those elements of social control which seemed cold and alien to the humanist perspective, and strove to shape us into something more suited to their own purposes, all the while denying the value of our essential humanity. Whether those powers be institutional, cultural, social-hierarchical, or personal, I thought their over-reach and impact would resonate with the experience of most Canadians.

That year, or the next, Reg suggested to me that he had written some short stories that could be adapted to this theme. I was busy trying to finish another novel ('The New Planet Policy') while also completing the educational and experience requirements toward professional certification for my full-time job. I had lost focus on this project, and so I offered it to him.

Reg would select from among the stories we received from hopeful writers, edit them, and also drive the cover design and book information development. Yes, I had a couple of stories to contribute, but I left it to his judgment as to how he would incorporate them into the final product. I was excited to perhaps finally have something within the Fresh Blue Ink offerings that was not all me.

Years passed with little apparent progress. I assumed he was not receiving many candidate stories from eager contributors. Finally, in 2024, just after releasing my current novel, I pivoted back to Reg for a project update. Yes, he told me, the book is almost ready. However, he had nothing he could show me right then, and I should ask again later.

I wasn't sure if perhaps he simply hadn't done the work and was hiding this fact, which is understandable (editing one's own work is hard enough, indeed Stephen King calls it "killing your babies"; I cannot imagine how difficult it might be to edit the work of others) or if there was some other reason he didn't want to show me what had been accomplished to that point.

After that I had two final phone calls with him. In the first, on March 1st, we set a plan to get together and jam the following Friday night. I briefly asked if he had the final manuscript yet, and he seemed to struggle for an answer. It was finished but it wasn't finished. He had contacted the authors; he had not contacted the authors. The blurb was written, but no, it wasn't ready to be seen. He seemed disturbed by my casual query and the phone call ended somewhat abruptly.

He did not arrive at the jam that Friday and instead sent a short text apologizing that something had come up and he just could not make it.

The last time I talked to him, he seemed quite changed. I asked about his non-arrival the previous Friday, and he laughed, rather inappropriately in my view. He seemed comically or condescendingly outraged that I should ask him to come to my place and have fun making music while the world was facing 'complete disintegration'.

He said my metaphor of the Space Lizard had become reality, or was reality somehow, that there were 'forces' we could not easily see or understand that were pulling the strings of reality, including not only world history, but each personal history as well. This sounded like conspiracy theory to me.

Reg is an imaginative fellow but he had never strayed into believing the truly incredible. In that final call, however, he expounded on other conspiracy theories (which I decline to list here) and how they might be related to the Space Lizard trope.

(Okay, I will mention one thing. He said that the American President was actually a Space Lizard and that he had come to Earth to take all of our eggs. Space Lizard civilization was failing; their pollution levels had rendered their own eggs non-viable. They needed healthy eggs to aid their own reproduction, and for some reason, chicken eggs from Earth were their best solution. Reg shared that his source had insisted that this was the reason for US egg shortages, not 'fake bird Covid'. This was ONE of several imaginative ideas Reg shared in his last phone call.)

I had always thought of the project theme as a metaphor wide enough to allow expression of all forms of protest and self-disclosure, but never as something real. It was as if I had asked people to submit fictional ghost stories with metaphoric allusions, but instead received true-life ghost reports. Instead of entertainment, it had become foolish faux journalism. I found our conversation unsettling and I admit I wondered about his pharmaceutical situation: too much or too little?

Unsettled by all this, I soon went to Reg's place to see how he was doing. I was shocked when his girlfriend Daffodil opened the door with tears in her eyes. That very morning he had left a strange note saying he would not allow powerful, unspecified forces to endanger his family or friends and therefore had to leave town. I was shocked but found some measure of reassurance in the fact that he had taken some of his belongings with him. This showed he intended to survive.

Daffodil gave me a folder of the Space Lizard story drafts and other papers, as well as, luckily, a USB stick containing the manuscript of the final versions of the stories contained in this present collection.

She also showed me his office, which was in a state. The physical evidence left behind made little sense. Some of the envelopes from the contributors are marked with far future dates. Even discounting the issue of time travel, who uses snail mail in the far future? So I must assume it is a joke.

Additionally, there exists software and printers easily capable of creating such artifacts as part of a hoax. The stories all seem to have one element in common, the titular Space Lizards. Why would he not alert me to these submissions? Many have no envelope and appear to have the same font and format despite being indicated as having different authors.

In his notes, I can read Reg had specified the order for the stories, and even had the cover ready, so that is what I used. Daffodil told me that Reg was excited and even grandiose about the project and was getting ready to unveil it at the time of his disappearance.

After looking more carefully at what was left behind in Reg's office, I see that many of these stories were changed substantially. Some of the original submissions didn't even mention Space Lizards at all! This goes far beyond a copy edit, or even a re-write; some of it is wilful re-purposing.

Nevertheless, I do see the merits of his story order

as a sequence amid crescendo, a gentle rising of the volume until they, those creatures, occupy our foreground. Reg knew the final project delivery date: June 14, 2025, the North Kanata Book Fair, so bearing in my mind a general good opinion of him, especially as per past promises kept, we will go forward with his version of the book.

Print!

*Final update*

Daffodil has told me more about who Reg was hanging out with just before he left. Apparently he was involved with a band called 'Green Alert!' who believed in something called the Anti-Human Agenda, which is supposedly a group of humans who smooth the way for the Space Lizards agenda: to infiltrate our planet. That sounds like a reliable group!

Anyway, not to worry; it is all very normal for an artistic bohemian like Reg to get surrounded by an idea with no retreat possible. Like most creative introverts, his imagination generates a set of images which represent the sum of his intuitive understanding of the world; he doesn't rely upon his sense data as most humans do, but rather takes an approach both intellectual and instinctual to orient himself.

This can lead to great insights and wonderfully entertaining ideas, but can also mislead him into paradox and disaster.

*Second final update*

I received a threatening message: make sure you
label your book as fiction. Wow and yikes. How did
they know about the book and its contents? Surely
this is someone Reg was in contact with and has
similarly wild ideas.

*Third final update*

Reg has re-surfaced! He has been appointed as
ambassador to the Space Lizards. They landed
yesterday.

Now I see the live stream. They are on the front
lawn of the White House and the President is
kneeling down in front of them, proffering
something on a tasselled, little golden cushion.

The President doesn't look very surprised. I admit I
have no idea wtf is happening.


THE END

www.ingramcontent.com/pod-product-compliance
Lightning Source LLC
Chambersburg PA
CBHW051926220626
47052CB00003B/590